LiTTLe FLOWeR

Gloria Rand

Illustrated by **R.W. Alley**

HENRY HOLT AND COMPANY
NEW YORK

Henry Holt and Company, LLC, *Publishers since 1866*
115 West 18th Street, New York, New York 10011

Henry Holt is a registered trademark of Henry Holt and Company, LLC
Text copyright © 2002 by Gloria Rand
Illustrations copyright © 2002 by R. W. Alley
All rights reserved. Distributed in Canada
by H. B. Fenn and Company Ltd.

Library of Congress Cataloging-in-Publication Data
Rand, Gloria.
Little Flower / Gloria Rand; pictures by R. W. Alley.
Summary: When Miss Pearl falls and breaks her hip, her potbellied
pig, Little Flower, goes for help.
[1. Pigs—Fiction. 2. Pets—Fiction. 3. Accidents—Fiction.]
I. Alley, R. W. (Robert W.), ill. II. Title.
PZ7.R1553Li 2001 [E]—dc21 00-40982

ISBN 0-8050-6480-X
First Edition—2002 / Book design by David Caplan
Printed in the United States of America on acid-free paper. ∞

10 9 8 7 6 5 4 3 2 1

illustrated

Dedicated to Sheila Horder,
a dear, dear friend and fellow writer
—G. R.

To Claudia Gordon, with thanks,
and to Cassandra, pig aficionado
—R. W. A.

Miss Pearl was very proud of Little Flower, her potbellied pig.

"Little Flower is so smart," Miss Pearl told her neighbors. "She has learned to do a funny trick. Watch.

"Play dead, Little Flower." Little Flower rolled onto her back and stuck her small feet straight up in the air.

"That's not at all funny," said Miss Pearl's next-door neighbor, Mr. Highchew. Mrs. Highchew was not amused either.

But the other neighbors thought that Little Flower's trick was very funny. They said she was quite a remarkable pig.

As for Little Flower, she quickly learned that whenever she wanted attention all she had to do was play dead.

One day Miss Pearl slipped
and fell on her kitchen floor.
She hurt her hip. She could
not get up.

"Help! Help!" she cried, but nobody
heard her. She was desperate. From where
she lay on the floor, Miss Pearl began to throw
whatever she could reach. She managed to break
out a window with a heavy candlestick. Now
maybe someone would hear her calling for help.

The crashing and calls for help frightened Little Flower. She headed for the old doggy door that she had used when she was a tiny piglet. Little Flower groaned and snorted as she tried to squeeze through the small opening.

Finally, bruised and tired, she managed to push
herself out the door. She flopped down on the front
porch, rolled onto her back, and played dead. Surely
someone would notice her. But no one did.

She tried again. This time Little
Flower played dead by the garden gate.
No one noticed her there either.

She hurried back into the house.
Miss Pearl was still lying on the floor.
Little Flower, huffing and puffing,
quickly went back outside.

Little Flower ran out into the middle of the street.

She played dead one more time.

A car screeched to a stop, and a young man got out.

"Hey! What's wrong?" he asked Little Flower, who had gotten to her feet. "I thought you were hurt. Does your owner know you're loose?"

Little Flower trotted back into Miss Pearl's garden. The young man followed. He knocked on the door.

"I'm in here. I need help!" Miss Pearl called in a weak voice.

The young man opened the door. There was Miss Pearl, lying on the floor. He covered her with a blanket and assured her that she was going to be fine. Then he dialed 9-1-1.

"I found a woman lying injured on her kitchen floor," he reported. "She lives in a small yellow cottage that's between Willow Way and Spruce Street. Please hurry!"

With lights flashing and siren howling, an ambulance arrived. The emergency medical technicians dashed inside.

Soon Miss Pearl's neighbors came running from every direction.

"What's going on?" Mr. Highchew asked. He was very upset.

"Why didn't Miss Pearl call one of us for help?" his wife asked.

Everyone wondered what the trouble was.

After a short time, Miss Pearl was wheeled out on a stretcher.

"Is she going to be all right?" several neighbors asked the technicians.

"Everything's okay" was their polite reply. "Please stand back."

"You too," one technician told Little Flower, who had flopped down as close to Miss Pearl's stretcher as she could get.

"Oh, Little Flower." Miss Pearl reached out to pat her pet pig. "I can't leave you."

"Yes, you can," Mr. Highchew said. "We'll all look after her until you come back home."

Taking care of Little
Flower was not that easy.

She missed Miss Pearl so
much she wouldn't eat,

not even jelly doughnuts,
which were her
favorite treat.

"Come on, cheer up," Mrs. Highchew said and offered Little Flower a chocolate candy. "Miss Pearl is getting better. She'll be coming home soon."

Of course Little Flower didn't understand what Mrs. Highchew was saying.

But a few days later, when
neighbors started to arrive at the
cottage with beautiful flowers and
delicious-smelling food, Little
Flower perked up.

She even trotted around happily
as other neighbors decorated the
front gate with colorful ribbons
and balloons.

"Let's dress you up with a ribbon too." Mrs.
Highchew tied a big bow around Little Flower's neck.
"You want to look your best for Miss Pearl's home-
coming, don't you?"

"Miss Pearl has always taken care of you. And when she needed help, you took care of her," Mr. Highchew told Little Flower. "You're a real hero."

All the neighbors smiled. They thought so too.

Little Flower stood proudly, waiting
for Miss Pearl to return. She certainly
was a remarkable pig.